To my loved ones, for believing in possibilities as we go forward at our own pace. To Pierson and Lyla, Always remember you have the abilities to be great!

Love You All

She is loved and cared for
In the grandest of style.

She loves to play with her dolls
Some big and some small.
They have tea and cookies
They're always having a ball!

The day is winding down
They have all been playing hard.
Mom calls out to Elsy
Time to come in from the yard.

It's bath time now
Let's all go to the tub.

Elsy's dolls sit on the edge of the tub
She has them all in single file.

But something goes wrong
That seem as big as a mile!

She drops her favorite doll
In the bath tub it went.
Full of soapy bubbles
It is starting to become a major event.

The bubbles are still floating
But her doll is now wet.
Things are starting to unravel
Poor Elsy is getting upset

Her parents do not know
What the fuss is about,
A doll fell into the water
We'll dry it and get the water out.

Elsy couldn't understand
What do they not see?

My favorite doll is ruined
It's a big deal to me!

Her parents explain
That these things can be fixed.

But being a kid,
Her world has just been nixed.

We'll dry it with warm air,
We hope you understand.

Things that are wet
Can be dried very quick.

Don't cry sweet girl,
It'll be done in a tick.

To her parents
There should not be any fuss.

So, remember that issues
Are not just what we see.

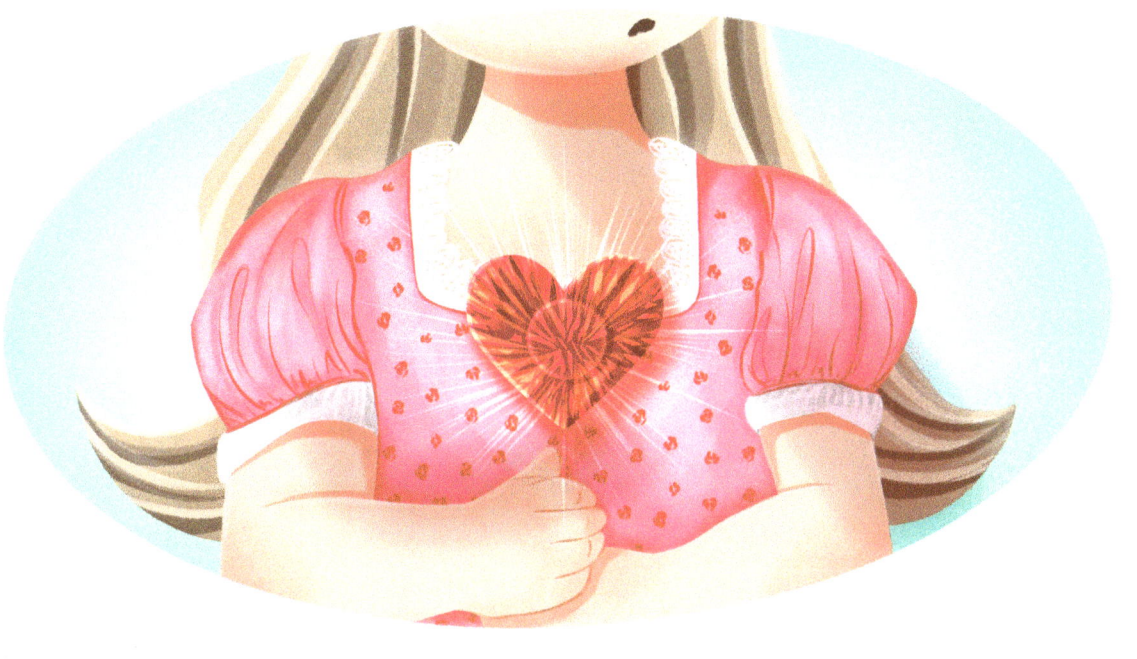

But what we feel inside
Is a big deal to me!

Printed in the USA
CPSIA information can be obtained
at www.ICGtesting.com
LVHW070551070224
771185LV00012B/295